Holly Takes a Risk

The Mermaid S.O.S. series

Holly Takes a Risk

gillian shields

illustrated by helen turner

BLOOMSBURY
CHILDREN'S
BOOKS

Oceania

Giant Kelp
Forest

Rocky Islands

Fishing
Nets

Shipwreck

N
E
W
S

First published in Great Britain in 2006 by Bloomsbury Publishing Plc.
Published in the United States in 2008 by Bloomsbury U.S.A. Children's Books
175 Fifth Avenue, New York, New York 10010
Distributed to the trade by Macmillan

Library of Congress Cataloging-in-Publication Data available upon request
ISBN-13: 978-1-59990-214-2 • ISBN-10: 1-59990-214-1

First U.S. Edition 2008
Printed in the U.S.A. by Quebecor World Fairfield
2 4 6 8 10 9 7 5 3 1

For Rhona, Sheena,
and Catriona
—G. S.

This book is for my lovely grandparents,
who have always encouraged me
to reach for the stars. All my love
—H. J.

Prologue

Meet Misty, Ellie, Sophie, Holly, Lucy, and Scarlett. They are Mermaid Sisters of the Sea, who live in the magical underwater world of Coral Kingdom. The Merfolk and their wise ruler, Queen Neptuna, look after the sea and all its creatures.

Coral Kingdom is protected by six powerful magic crystals, which give life and strength to the Merfolk.

Without the crystals, Coral Kingdom would not survive.

Every year, the old crystals fade and have to be replaced. Queen Neptuna sends Misty and her friends—six special mermaids who are pure of heart—to collect the new ones from the secret Crystal Cave. But as they are bringing the crystals home, a storm blows the mermaids completely off course.

This is no ordinary storm! It is created by Mantora, Queen Neptuna's jealous sister. Mantora wanted to rule Coral Kingdom, and now she is bitter and full of hatred. She is determined to stop the mermaids from returning home, so that she can overthrow Queen Neptuna and set up her evil Storm Kingdom instead.

Luckily, the young mermaids have courage and friendship on their side. But that's not all; their S.O.S. Kits will help them as they race to get the crystals back safely. And they never forget their Mermaid Pledge:

We promise that we'll take good care
Of all sea creatures everywhere.
We'll never hurt and never break,
We'll always give and never take.
And as we fight Mantora's threat,
This saying we must not forget:
"I'll help you and you'll help me,
For we are Sisters of the Sea!"

Holly and her friends are eager to prove that Queen Neptuna was right to trust them with the precious crystals. They are going to do everything it takes to get them home and safeguard Coral Kingdom for another year.

Will Mantora win? Or can the mermaids get the new crystals back in time to stop the light fading forever from Coral Kingdom?

Holly

Chapter One

The sun was setting in a blaze of gold over the sea. The mermaids Holly, Misty, Ellie, Sophie, Lucy, and Scarlett had been swimming west with their new friends the dolphins. Earlier in the day, they had rescued one of them, Silver, who had been tangled in a fishing net. Now Silver and her sisters were changing course to head for their home in the Wild Waves. They called "farewell" to the mermaids by leaping high over the water in a shower of golden droplets.

"Good-bye, Sisters of the Sea!" called Silver. "I'll never forget that you saved my life."

"Thank you, mermaids," cried her baby, Smudge, waving his soft flippers and smiling

with his snuffly beak. Then he dashed
happily after his mother as the dolphin
family sped toward the far horizon.

"It was exciting to swim with Silver
and her sisters," said Holly, swishing her
yellow tail gently in the cool sea. "But we
should rest now. We're all tired, and
Lucy can barely stay awake."

"I can keep going," said Lucy bravely. "We must get closer to Coral Kingdom."

Queen Neptuna had asked the courageous young mermaids to fetch six new crystals for her silver Throne. If Holly and her friends didn't get them home by the end of the week, the power of the Merfolk would fade forever. But Coral Kingdom still lay far ahead in the West.

"We can't continue swimming without stopping, Lucy," said Misty, "even though we'd like to."

"Misty's right," agreed Sophie. "Tomorrow there will still be three days left before the old crystals fade. We can take a short break."

"I think we'll have to," yawned Ellie, "if we can find a place to sleep."

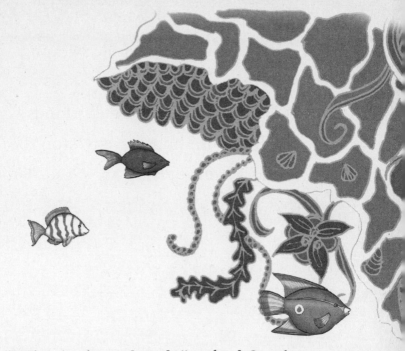

"What's that ahead?" asked Scarlett, pointing in front of her.

Holly looked over the waves in the gathering dusk. She could see some dark buoys bobbing up and down in the water, topped by flickering warning lights. Beyond them, a string of green mounds rose gently from the sea in the twilight.

They were crowned by small, swaying trees.

"It looks like a group of reef islands," Holly said. "Those buoys are to stop the human boats from getting too close. That will be a perfect place to rest."

"As long as Mantora isn't hanging around," muttered Scarlett. "Nowhere is safe while she's trying to stop us from getting the crystals home."

The friends set off with weary limbs toward the reef islands. The moon sailed high in the sky and the sea sparkled silver. They swam past the bobbing buoys and saw the shape of the reef spread out below them in the clear, shallow water.

"This reminds me of Coral Kingdom," said Misty. "I think we really must be getting closer now."

"Of course!" said Holly suddenly. "I know exactly where we must be. And I know a story about these islands—an old legend."

"Ooh, what? Tell us, Holly!" cried the others eagerly. They knew Holly was very smart and had learned lots of things about the ocean from Queen Neptuna's sea scrolls.

"Let's settle down for the night, then I'll tell you all about it," she replied with a smile.

The mermaids quickly chose a small, deserted island with a soft white beach. They pulled themselves out of the water and sat in a circle on the glistening sand. Lucy found her Mermaid Comb in the dainty green pouch tied around her waist, and she combed her friends' shining hair in turn. The cool night breeze ruffled their silky curls as the stars began to glitter in the velvety sky.

"What about that story now, Holly?" said Ellie drowsily.

"Yes, please," begged the others, stifling

their yawns as they snuggled down to rest. They looked at Holly with expectant, sleepy eyes. "Tell us a bedtime story, but don't make it a scary one!"

It was good to be quiet after such a busy day. Listening to a story reminded the mermaids of being at home with their families.

Holly smiled at her friends, took a deep breath, and began.

Chapter Two

"These reef islands are called the Shipwreck Isles," said Holly. "I've seen them on Queen Neptuna's great map, which hangs in her palace. Coral Kingdom lies beyond them, further to the West."

"Why are they called the Shipwreck Isles?" asked Misty.

"That's all part of the legend," replied Holly. "You saw the coral reef under the waves. It's dangerous for the humans to sail their boats too close to the sharp peaks and pinnacles of the coral, so there are warning lights on those buoys out there. But even so, there have been many wrecks in these waters."

"I feel sorry for the humans who are shipwrecked," said tender-hearted Lucy. "This sounds like a sad story, Holly."

"The next part isn't sad at all," Holly reassured her. "It's about the most famous shipwreck of all, the *Lady Jane*."

"That sounds like a fine, elegant ship," said Ellie.

"It was," answered Holly. "The legend goes that the *Lady Jane* made her voyage here more than two hundred years ago. She had three tall masts, billowing white sails, and a splendid gilded prow. It was carved in the shape of a . . ."

". . . a mermaid!" guessed Sophie and Scarlett at the same time, laughing together.

"That's right." Holly grinned. "The

carved mermaid had a curling golden tail and long fair hair, but her sweet smiling face was a portrait of the ship owner's wife, the real Lady Jane. Her husband, Sir Richard, had worked hard to make his fortune in the prosperous lands near here. At last, he had sent his ship to bring Lady Jane and their children to join him in his new life."

"So what happened?" asked Misty, with big, wondering eyes.

"A terrible storm sprang up as the *Lady Jane* reached these islands. The ship grounded on the reef, and everyone's lives were in danger."

"How dreadful," whispered Lucy.

"Ah, but help wasn't far away," Holly continued. "The Merfolk heard the

pitiful cries of the young mother, and saw
the golden mermaid prow plunging in the
billowing waves. Lady Jane was clutching
the ship's rails, with her children clinging
to her skirts. She was weeping, saying
that she didn't care if she sank to the
bottom of the sea, as long as her children
were spared."

31

"Poor lady," said Ellie. "She must have been so frightened."

"Her gentleness and beauty filled the hearts of the Merfolk with pity," added Holly. "They rescued Lady Jane and everyone else before the ship sank, carrying them to these islands, where they were found safe and well the next day."

"But what did the humans say when they saw the Merfolk?" asked Misty. "They must have thought they were dreaming!"

"The sailors babbled afterward that a band of angels had snatched them from the storm," laughed Holly. "Of course, nobody believed them. But Lady Jane always declared that a mermaid had saved

her children's lives, and she showed her gratitude in a special way."

"How?" asked the friends eagerly. "What did she do?"

"When she was reunited with Sir Richard," said Holly, "Lady Jane asked him to bring her back here on another boat. Then she cast her little ruby earrings overboard as a thank you gift to the Merfolk. My granny told me that Lady Jane's rubies are still lying on the seabed, near the ghostly wreck of her proud ship."

"Ooh, how exciting!" said the others. "That's a great story."

"But is it just a story?" wondered Holly. "Wouldn't it be amazing if we actually saw the *Lady Jane* tomorrow? We could

even find one of the rubies and take it home for Queen Neptuna!"

"The only things Queen Neptuna wants us to take home are the crystals," said Scarlett sensibly. "We can't risk spending time looking for ghost ships, Holly."

"But couldn't we just take a peep on our way home tomorrow?" Holly pleaded. Her head was full of legends, stories, and treasure, so for once she wasn't being her usual cautious self.

"I suppose it would be fun to look," said Misty. "If you're really sure it won't make us late."

"It won't!" promised Holly. "We have to swim over the reef anyway to head for Coral Kingdom. What do you all think?"

"Well, all right," agreed Scarlett. "But

we'll have to get up extra early, so that we
don't lose too much time on our journey
home with the crystals."

"I'll wake everyone as soon as the sun
rises," said Holly excitedly. The mermaids
murmured good night to each other. Lucy

began to sing a gentle lullaby in her sweet, soft voice:

> *Here is the end*
> *Of this bright day,*
> *Tomorrow we must*
> *Be on our way.*
> *But now we'll rest*
> *And meet our dreams,*
> *Beneath the stars*
> *And soft moonbeams . . .*

Soon the mermaid friends drifted off to sleep.

But Holly was restless. Muddled dreams raced through her head of ships, rubies, and adventures as the waves lapped all night long on the silvery shore.

Chapter Three

Holly thought she was still dreaming when a wild seabird cried out to greet the dawn. She opened her eyes sleepily. The pale light of the sun was starting to break through the soft clouds. Then she remembered. The mermaids were on the reef island, and they were going to look for the wreck of the *Lady Jane*!

"It's the new day, everyone," Holly called, as she sat up.

The young friends slowly uncurled their sparkling tails and stretched.

"We're heading for Coral Kingdom today," Holly said excitedly. "And who knows—maybe we'll see the old shipwreck."

The mermaids quickly got ready to

leave. They checked that their magical crystals were hidden safely in their pouches, and soon they were swimming out toward the reef, eager to be on their way. But Holly suddenly slowed down and looked around carefully.

"That's strange," she said to her friends, as they rippled their bright tails through the fresh waves. "Something looks different."

"Maybe that's because we're seeing the reef islands by daylight now," suggested Ellie.

Holly hovered in the water for a moment, searching the waves with her keen dark eyes.

"Hmm, I'm not sure," she said. "Something has definitely changed since last night . . ."

"Are you worried, Holly?" asked Lucy, in a concerned voice. "Should we stop?"

"Nooo . . . ," Holly replied slowly. "I'm probably just imagining it. Come on, we'll risk it. Follow me!"

She flicked her yellow tail and dived under the satiny sea in a splash of foam. Her friends swiftly followed. They were all thrilled by the sight of the magnificent coral reef, stretching out in the clear water below them.

"Oh, it's so much like Coral Kingdom," cried Lucy gladly. "Look, there are turtles!"

"Parrot fish!" said Ellie.

"Shrimps!" said Sophie.

"Angelfish!" said Misty.

"And look at those gorgeous fronds of red seaweed," said Holly. "They're as bright as Scarlett's tail!"

The colorful coral was full of life. Some
of the reef dwellers were just starting to
wake up, and others were going to bed
after a busy night. They watched curiously

as the mermaids swam past, swishing their sparkling tails and making trails of silver bubbles.

"I wonder where we should look for the shipwreck," said Holly, weaving in and out of the twisting branches of coral.

"Don't forget that we're just going to swim over the reef without stopping," said Scarlett. "We can't go out of our way for treasure hunting!"

"I know, Scarlett," smiled Holly. "I promise I won't do anything to put our crystals or our journey in danger. I just think it would be fun to see the shipwreck—if it really exists."

"If?" said a slow, deep voice behind them. "If? Are you saying that you don't believe the legend of the Shipwreck Isles?"

Holly and her friends whirled around in the water. A large green turtle with a dappled shell, strong flippers, and a comical face was eyeing them very closely.

"I beg your pardon," gasped Holly. "We've heard of the legend, of course, but we weren't sure if it was real."

"Of course it's real," said the turtle sternly. Then he smiled. "My name is

Tobias. I have lived here for many years, and my family before me, going all the way back to the time of dear Lady Jane herself. I can show you the wreck of her ship if you like."

"Can you really?" exclaimed Holly. "That is, if it wouldn't take too long. We're on an important journey for Queen Neptuna," she explained hurriedly.

"Well, well, we can't delay royal business," replied Tobias. "This will only take a minute."

Holly looked at the others excitedly. "Should we?"

"Oh, let's go and see it," said Misty. "Just a quick peek can't do any harm."

"Then follow me," said the turtle, gliding ahead of them in the clear water.

The young friends surged after him,
curving around the spiky walls of the reef.
After a little while, the strangest sight
loomed up below them. On the bottom of
the sandy seabed, lying on its keel, was
the ghostly skeleton of a once splendid

ship. Its three great masts reached upward into the water like slim trees in a winter forest. The tattered remains of the sails fluttered in the current like a few forlorn leaves.

"Oh, it's so sad and beautiful," breathed the mermaids. They swam closer and saw the name LADY JANE in faded red paint on the wooden side. At the front of the ship, the carved mermaid prow still gleamed golden, though the face was chipped and worn.

"So it was all true," said Lucy softly. The young friends gazed for a moment in awe at the gallant, derelict ship, and thought about the brave souls who had sailed with her.

"Was it worth coming to see?" asked Holly in a whisper.

"Definitely!" the others replied.

"I've heard that the Merfolk from the old times left Lady Jane's rubies lying in the sea nearby," added Tobias. "They said that mermaids would come back here to find the jewels one day. I don't know whether that part of the story is true. But at least you can see that the wreck is true, as real as you and me!"

"Thank you so much for showing it to us, Tobias," said Holly gratefully, tearing herself away from the silent, shadowy ship. "But we really do have to speed on our way now. Would you kindly lead us in the direction of Coral Kingdom?"

"Certainly, my dears," he replied. "It's been a pleasure to have some of the Merfolk by our reef once more."

The gentle turtle led them up to the sparkling surface of the sea just above the tips of the coral reef. Holly and her friends shook the drops of water from their shining hair and turned their thoughts to getting home with the crystals. They listened carefully as Tobias gave them directions.

"To go west you need to follow . . . ," the

turtle began, but he never finished what he was saying.

A black cloud passed over the sun and everything went dark. Then a blast of icy wind whipped over the mermaids' shoulders, and the sea began to crash menacingly around them.

"Something's happening!" cried Misty.

The waves suddenly swelled into green mountains of water, and out of nowhere a

human boat loomed over the friends like
a menacing shadow. Tobias and the
mermaids instantly dived under the huge
waves out of sight, but not before Holly
saw a man staggering by the wheel of the
boat. He was desperately trying to regain
control as the sea raged up and down.

It was too late. The bottom of the boat
ripped against the sharp peaks of the reef
with a sickly crunch. Water began to gush

into it. Holly heard hideous cackling laughter floating through the swirling wind and sea.

"Mantora!" she cried to her friends. "She's here somewhere!"

Chapter Four

The boat lurched over onto its side. Holly
and the other mermaids clung to each
other under the crashing waves. More peals
of triumphant laughter echoed around and
filled them with horror.

Above the freakish waves, the terrified
man was struggling to release the
inflatable life raft that was stored on deck.
After a last frantic effort, he managed to

climb on to the raft and get out of the way of the sinking boat. With trembling hands, he sent up a bright red emergency flare. It blazed high over the sky like fire from a volcano. All he had to do now was wait for the next passing boat to find him, and he would be safe, though with a terrible tale to tell.

A tremendous noise deafened the mermaids as the man's damaged craft finally tipped right over, sucked down into the churning sea. As it sank, six large, barrel-like canisters fell from the boat and knocked against the side of the reef. They startled all the fish from their hiding places like a cloud of silver butterflies. The canisters thundered down, down, down, and the boat landed with a

heart-stopping thump on the seabed.

There was an uneasy silence. The wind and the waves gradually returned to normal. The young friends looked around, relieved that none of them had been hurt. Tobias was quaking in his shell next to them. The mermaids glided nervously over the coral, peering down at the newly sunken boat.

"Well," said Scarlett, in a shaky voice, "you wanted to see a shipwreck, Holly. Now we really have!"

"It was horrible," shuddered Holly. "And I'm sure Mantora was the cause of it, trying to wreck our mission."

The others murmured in agreement.

"I'm glad the man got away," said Lucy, "but why was he steering his boat so close to the reef? Didn't he see the warning buoys?"

"That's it!" cried Holly suddenly. "The warning buoys! That's what was different when we set off for the reef this morning—they were missing. Someone must have removed all the buoys that told the boats to keep away from the sharp coral."

"Who would have done such a thing?" asked Ellie.

"Mantora!" replied the others, with a groan.

"Let's think," said Holly quickly. "Why would Mantora have attacked that particular boat? What was it carrying?"

"I can tell you that," said Tobias. "Look at those big barrels down there. The humans often take them far out to sea and dump them. Then they lie forgotten at the bottom of the ocean. But the barrels are full of poisonous waste that the humans don't want on the land. It's called chemi . . . oh, chemi-something . . ."

"Chemicals?" suggested smart Holly.

"That's the word I was looking for," said Tobias. "The humans aren't supposed to throw these containers into the sea, but some selfish people do it anyway."

Holly and the others peered down to where the shiny metal canisters lay on the seabed near the wrecked boat. They had strange markings on them.

"Let's go take a look," said Holly determinedly.

"Be careful," warned Misty. Then Holly

turned to her with a very serious look on her face.

"I took a silly risk because I wanted to see the *Lady Jane*," she said, "but I'm not going to let anything bad happen to Tobias and the reef because of my mistakes. I don't trust Mantora one little bit, and I want to see what she was up to."

"We'd better come with you," said Ellie. "We are a team after all."

Holly squeezed Ellie's hand gratefully, then swooped down to the seabed with a flick of her yellow tail. The others swam near to her, with Tobias slowly following behind.

When the friends got closer to the metal containers, they could see what the marks were. Two thick lines formed an "x" shape

with a round blob in
the middle.

"The skull and
crossbones!" gasped
Scarlett.

"That's the sign for
poison and danger,"
said Lucy anxiously.

"And it means that Tobias was right,"
explained Holly. "These canisters contain
chemicals that the humans wanted to
dump far out at sea. But they've landed
here by the reef because of Mantora's
cunning plot—and look!"

She pointed urgently to the heavy metal
barrels. Thin jets of black liquid were
escaping from two of them, clouding the
water with their filmy darkness.

"They're leaking!" exclaimed Misty. "Those two containers must have been punctured when they crashed against the sharp coral."

The mermaids peered down at where the dark liquid spurted out. Both of those barrels had a tiny round hole punched in their metal sides. Sophie started to cough.

"This water is beginning to taste bad," she spluttered. "The chemicals are spoiling it already."

"Move away, everyone," shouted Scarlett.

Tobias and the mermaids shot away from the wrecked boat and the canisters. From a safe distance, they watched the black liquid slowly seeping into the beautiful clear water around the reef.

"If we don't do something soon to plug

up those holes," said Misty, "all the poison
will escape."

"And this part of the reef will die,"
added Tobias miserably. "Our beautiful

red seaweed will wither away. There'll be no food for the fish and the other creatures. We turtles have lived here for so many years, but now our home will be destroyed!"

Holly looked at her friends with flaming cheeks, burning with shame. She bowed her head.

"This is all my fault," she said. "I'm so sorry."

Chapter Five

"We don't think that it's your fault, Holly," said Misty quickly. "Do we, everyone?"

"Of course not," soothed Ellie. "Mantora might have attacked that boat even if we hadn't visited the *Lady Jane*."

"I don't think so," said Holly unhappily. "She must have overheard us talking on the island last night and then planned all this. She's trying to stop us from getting home with the crystals again. Oh, Scarlett, you warned me that stopping to see the shipwreck would be a risk."

"I could have persuaded you not to, if I'd really tried," Scarlett replied ruefully. "But I secretly wanted to see the *Lady Jane*, too. We're all to blame—or none of us!"

"It doesn't matter who's to blame," said Lucy. "The important thing is how to stop the black liquid from hurting the plants and creatures who live here."

"And then getting back on track with our mission," added Sophie.

"You're right," said Holly, looking at her

friends' kind faces. "That is the important thing. Ideas, anyone?"

"Could we drag the canisters onto one of the islands?" asked Misty. The others glanced up hopefully. It seemed like a good suggestion.

"I'm not sure that we'd be able to move them," Sophie replied slowly. "They look really heavy. And we don't want the poison leaking out on a reef island either. That could harm the crabs and birds there."

"If we can't move those two containers," said Holly, "I think the best thing would be to plug up the holes somehow. Then the liquid can't escape."

"Good idea," said Sophie, "but how can we plug them up?"

The mermaids eagerly searched through their S.O.S. Kits, looking for something useful. Tucked away in a corner of her purple pouch, Ellie found a piece of dried seaweed. At the end of it was a small round pod, like a bead filled with air.

"Perhaps we could use something like this seaweed pod," she said. "Something small and round that would fit into the puncture holes."

"A seaweed pod full of air wouldn't be strong enough, though," Misty

70

replied. "It would have to be something hard and solid, something that was going to last forever . . ."

". . . something like a precious jewel," interupted Holly with a shout. "A ruby stone—Lady Jane's rubies!"

The young friends looked at each other with new hope.

"Do you really think we could find them in time?" asked Scarlett.

"The legend says that they lie near the wreck," said Tobias urgently. "That's what we turtles have always been told. I'll make sure that no creature swims near these leaking barrels, while you go and search for the rubies. Hurry, mermaids—and good luck!"

Holly led the way as the mermaids

surged back along the reef to where the wreck of the *Lady Jane* lay half-buried in the sandy seabed. As they saw its eerie masts lying ahead of them, the determined young friends swept into action, searching all over the seabed for the glinting jewels. But there was no sign of them anywhere.

"They must have fallen under the sand," groaned Misty. "We'll never find them in time."

"We'll just have to examine every grain of sand," said Scarlett stubbornly. "We're not going to give up."

Ellie and Lucy found some empty scallop shells in their S.O.S. Kits. The mermaids

used them to scoop up the glistening sand, then let it fall slowly through the clear water, trying to spot any flashes of red. But after scooping the sand over and over again, they felt discouraged.

"I'm afraid it's hopeless," said Sophie. "Even if we looked for a year and a day there'd always be another patch of the seabed to sift through."

"Maybe the answer doesn't lie there," said Holly thoughtfully. She looked up at the ghostly rigging of the submerged ship. "Maybe the rubies are hidden on the ship itself."

The mermaids swam cautiously toward the gray hulk of the wreck. They drifted through the old masts and rigging, examining it carefully. Then Sophie swooped down to the deck with a flick of her orange tail.

"Look," she said, "we could get through these broken deck planks into the ship's cabin."

The mermaids peered through the gaping hole. It was very dark inside and silent. They could just barely make out strange shapes in the gloom.

"We'll need our crystals to give us some light," said Holly bravely. "I'm going in!"

The others squeezed through the gap after her, clutching their gleaming crystals. Glimmering light flickered around the sunken cabin, and great shadows sprang up and wavered on the walls.

"It's so spooky," gulped Lucy.

"I think I've found something!" whispered Scarlett. She shone her crystal over an ancient-looking chest in a dark corner. The lid was studded with rusty iron nails and was propped open slightly.

"That would be the perfect place to keep long-lost treasure," breathed Ellie.

The mermaids gathered around, their hearts beating wildly, as Holly slowly lifted the creaking lid . . .

"Aaah!" They all squealed in fright. A

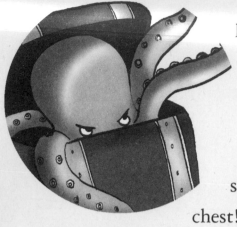

large, angry octopus shot out his snaky tentacles, startled from his sleep in the old chest! The mermaids dashed wildly out of the dark cabin into the clear sea.

"Ooof!" gasped Misty with relief.

"I've never been so frightened in my life," confessed Ellie, as the friends hovered by the wreck and watched the angry octopus swim away. "But we must try to find the jewels."

"I've just remembered something," said Holly quickly. "Tobias told us that the Merfolk in the old days said that mermaids would come back for the jewels at some time in the future. Well, what if those mermaids were actually us?"

"What do you mean, Holly?" asked Lucy in a puzzled voice.

"Some of the Merfolk are seers—they can see into the future," Holly reminded her. "Maybe the mermaids who rescued Lady Jane could see that we would come along one day, needing her rubies! If they did know that, where would they leave them?"

"In a place where we'd look for her jewels," murmured Lucy, with a strange expression on her face. "Oh, of course . . ."

She suddenly

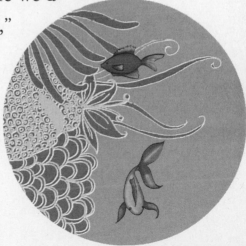

darted toward the prow of the shipwreck, followed swiftly by Holly and the others. They clustered excitedly around the old carved mermaid. And there, on the cracked and faded head were . . .

"The rubies!" cried Holly. "Lady Jane's statue is still wearing her earrings! Good job, Lucy."

Holly carefully reached forward and unhooked the delicate jewels from where they dangled on the painted ears of the figurehead.

"Thank you, Merfolk of the old times," she whispered. "We came for the rubies, just like you said. And thank you, Lady Jane."

Then the mermaids gasped. A trick of the light made it look as though the carved face smiled at them for a second.

"I think Lady Jane is pleased," said Lucy softly. "She wants us to have her jewels to save the reef."

"Then let's go and save it," cried Holly. "We'll swim back to Tobias with the rubies, everyone, before it's too late. *Mermaid S.O.S.!*"

Chapter Six

The young friends swooped eagerly through the water, away from the old-fashioned wreck toward the new and much more dangerous one. Tobias was waiting for them with two other turtles under a ledge on the coral reef.

"These are my kinsfolk, Tara and Titus," said Tobias. "I warned them not to swim across this part of the reef until you had plugged up the leak. Did you have any success?"

"We found the rubies," replied the mermaids triumphantly. They swirled to a halt and looked down at the broken boat. The dark jets seeping out into the water from the two punctured containers had grown stronger. A black cloud of gassy liquid hung over the wreck.

"I'll go down and try to plug the rubies into the holes," said Holly bravely. Then she dived toward the ominous metal barrels with the skull and crossbones on their gleaming sides.

"Wait," called Ellie. "You can't breathe in any of the bad water."

But Holly was already

choking and spluttering as she tried to get near the holes in the containers. She turned and sped back to her friends.

"I couldn't get close enough," she coughed, her eyes red and stinging. "But I have to plug up the holes or the poison will leak everywhere!"

A little crowd of worried creatures had gathered near the turtles, peering around the colorful branches of coral and the waving crimson seaweed. There was a squid, a family of boxer crabs, and some brilliant blue-green parrot fish.

"What's that horrible black cloud?" they muttered anxiously. "We've heard that the whole reef is going to be destroyed."

"Stay calm, everyone. These mermaids are going to save our reef," Tobias explained in a loud voice. "They are being helped by Lady Jane herself!"

Relieved murmurs quickly rippled around the little throng, followed by, "The mermaids are going to save our reef! They're going to save the reef!"

"*If* we can think of a way to get down to

the canisters without being poisoned ourselves," whispered Sophie, looking over at the bright parrot fish.

"Parrot fish!" cried Holly, following Sophie's gaze. "That's given me an idea. Parrot fish wrap themselves in a thick cocoon to keep themselves safe at night. That's what I need—a protective covering to keep me safe."

"Take my silk handkerchief," urged Scarlett, quickly searching in her S.O.S. Kit.

Holly wrapped the handkerchief over her face like a mask, then dashed back down to the canisters. She dropped the glinting rubies into the holes with her nimble fingers. The jewels fit exactly, and soon the hissing leaks came to a stop.

"Now we need to clear away the poison

that has already seeped out," she called to her friends. "It's time to use our crystals!"

The mermaids hovered a little distance

away from the cloud of discolored water, holding out their bright crystals. Brilliant red shafts of light, like tongues of flame, flowed from them and attacked the black liquid. For a moment, there seemed to be a great burning ring in the water. Then the flames and the dark cloud of poison disappeared, leaving nothing but the beautiful clear sea.

Finally, Holly placed her crystal on both the rubies in turn. They glowed a brilliant fire-red, like molten lava, then there was a flash of golden light.

"The rubies have been sealed in the containers by Mermaid Magic," she declared to Tobias and the other creatures. "Now they will never let a single drop of the black liquid leak over the reef. The red

seaweed, the coral, and the fish are all safe—and so are the turtles."

"Hooray!" cheered Tobias and the others. "We will cover this smashed boat and these ugly canisters with sand. Then no one will ever know that there was a new wreck at the Shipwreck Isles. And," he added, with a twinkle in his eye, "you mermaids have proved that our legend is true."

"I don't think I'll be searching for any

more ships from stories for
a long time," smiled
Holly. "It's just too
much of a risk!" Then she
looked serious again.

"I'm so sorry, everyone," she said, turning
to her friends. "I'm glad we found Lady
Jane's rubies to save the reef, but all this has
meant a long delay to our journey home."

"Don't worry," said the kindly green
turtle. "We can show you the fast currents
that lead to your Coral Kingdom. You'll
soon be making up for lost time."

"Oh, thank you so much, Tobias," said
the relieved mermaids. "You've been such
a good friend."

Holly and the others hid their crystals
away and swirled their sparkling tails.

Another long swim into the west lay ahead
of them.

The brave young Crystal Keepers were so
glad that Mantora hadn't been able to
wreck the reef or their vital journey home.

But the mermaids didn't know when or where she would be lurking next. It was going to take all their strength and courage to get the precious crystals back to Coral Kingdom in time.

Holly took a deep breath and plunged after Tobias and the turtles.

"Come on, Sisters of the Sea," she called. "Let's go!"

Mermaid Sisters of the Sea

Misty has flowing blonde hair and a shimmering pink tail. Misty is a really determined and brave mermaid.

Ellie is very caring and loves seabirds. She has long, wavy dark hair and a glittering purple tail.

Sophie has funky fair hair and a blazing, bright orange tail, which helps her to swim super fast.

Holly has sweet, short black hair and a dazzling yellow tail. Holly is very thoughtful and clever.

Scarlett has fabulous, thick dark hair and a gleaming red tail. She can be a little bit bossy and headstrong sometimes.

Lucy has fiery red hair and an emerald green tail, but don't let that fool you—she is really quite shy.

Read all the books in the Mermaid S.O.S. series!

Misty to the Rescue

gillian shields

Ellie and the Secret Potion

gillian shields

Sophie Makes a Splash

gillian shields

Holly Takes a Risk

gillian shields

Scarlett's New Friend

gillian shields

Lucy and the Magic Crystal

gillian shields